A Beginning-to-Read Book

A Friend for Dear Dragon

by Margaret Hillert

Illustrated by David Helton

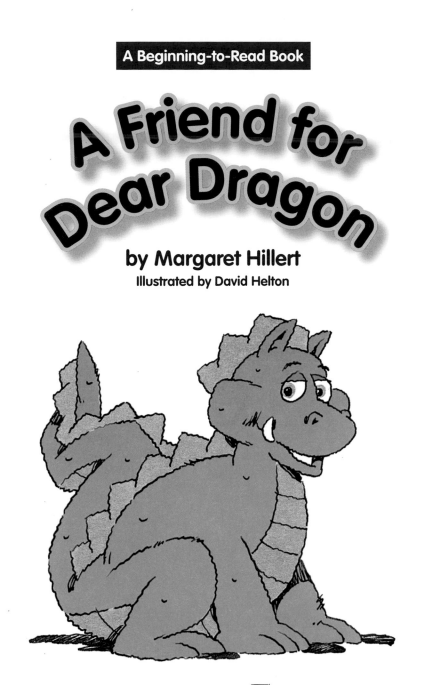

NORWOOD HOUSE PRESS

DEAR CAREGIVER,

The *Beginning-to-Read* series is a carefully written collection of classic readers you may remember from your own childhood. Each book features text comprised of common sight words to provide your child ample practice reading the words that appear most frequently in written text. The many additional details in the pictures enhance the story and offer the opportunity for you to help your child expand oral language and develop comprehension.

Begin by reading the story to your child, followed by letting him or her read familiar words and soon your child will be able to read the story independently. At each step of the way, be sure to praise your reader's efforts to build his or her confidence as an independent reader. Discuss the pictures and encourage your child to make connections between the story and his or her own life. At the end of the story, you will find reading activities and a word list that will help your child practice and strengthen beginning reading skills.

Above all, the most important part of the reading experience is to have fun and enjoy it!

Shannon Cannon

Shannon Cannon,
Literacy Consultant

Norwood House Press • P.O. Box 316598 • Chicago, Illinois 60631
For more information about Norwood House Press please visit our website at
www.norwoodhousepress.com or call 866-565-2900.

LIBRARY OF CONGRESS CATALOGING-IN-PUBLICATION DATA

Hillert, Margaret.
  A friend for dear dragon / by Margaret Hillert ; illustrated by David
Helton. — Rev. and expanded library ed.
    p. cm. — (Beginning to read series. Dear dragon)
  Summary: A boy and his pet dragon make friends with their new neighbors—
a girl and her unicorn. Includes reading activities.
  ISBN-13: 978-1-59953-016-1 (library ed. : alk. paper)
  ISBN-10: 1-59953-016-3 (library ed. : alk. paper)
  1. Readers (Primary) [1. Readers.] I. Helton, David, ill. II. Title. III. Series.
PE1119.H57858 2006
  428.6—dc22   2005034282

Beginning-to-Read series © 2006 by Margaret Hillert.
Library edition published by permission of Pearson Education, Inc. in arrangement
with Norwood House Publishing Company. All rights reserved.

Come here.
Come here.
I want you to see something.

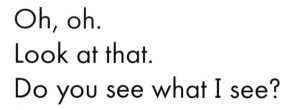

Oh, oh.
Look at that.
Do you see what I see?

4

Oh, now I see.
Here he comes with
something for that house.

Here comes a car.
Who is in it?
Can you see
who is in it?

Oh, oh.
It looks like a
friend for me.
Good, good.

And look, look.
A friend for you, too.
What a pretty
little one.

11

Come on.
Come on.
Here we go.
Out, out, out.

We are happy to see you.
You look like friends for us.
That is good.
We can play and have fun.

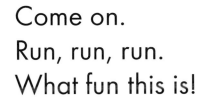

Come on.
Run, run, run.
What fun this is!

17

Now, look at this.
See what we two can do.
We like to play like this.

See, see.
He is good at this.
Look what he can do.

Yes, yes.
I see.
I see.
But we can do a good thing, too.

Look at that.
Did you see that?
That is good, too.

Look here.
This is not good.
No, no.
It is not good.

We two can help.
Get to work.
We can do this and this.
It will go in here.

Oh, my.
You are a big help, too.
You can get it for us.

We did good work.
Now, look here.
Look what we can have.

Oh, how good this is.
We like to eat this.
We are happy.

We are happy to have friends.
But we have to go home now.

Here you are with me.
And here I am with you.
Oh, it is good to have
friends, dear dragon.

The following activities support the findings of the National Reading Panel that determined the most effective components for reading instruction are: Phonemic Awareness, Phonics, Vocabulary, Fluency, and Text Comprehension.

Phonemic Awareness: The /f/ sound

Oral Blending: Say the beginning and ending sounds of the following words and ask your child to listen to the sounds and say the whole word:

/f/ + /ish/ = fish	/f/ + /eel/ = feel	/f/ + /ire/ = fire
/f/ + /ar/ = far	/f/ + /ast/ = fast	/f/ + /an/ = fan
/f/ + /un/ = fun	/f/ + /or/ = for	/f/ + /ood/ = food
/f/ + /eather/ = feather		

Phonics: The letter Ff

1. Demonstrate how to form the letters **F** and **f** for your child.

2. Have your child practice writing **F** and **f** at least three times each.

3. Ask your child to point to the words in the book that start with the letter **f**.

4. Write down the following words and ask your child to circle the letter **f** in each word:

fun	frog	family	coffee	flag	friend	leaf
raft	fan	sift	for	craft	roof	lift

Vocabulary: Related Words

1. Explain to your child that some words have many forms but the meanings are all related.

2. Write the following words on a piece of paper and explain how they are related and different, along with giving examples of each word in a sentence:

friend   friendly   friendship   befriend

3. Ask your child to describe the following:

- A time when someone was friendly to you . . .
- What you do to be a good friend . . .
- Things you do to keep your friendship . . .
- How you might befriend a new child at school or in the neighborhood . . .

Fluency: Shared Reading

1. Reread the story to your child at least two more times while your child tracks the print by running a finger under the words as they are read. Ask your child to read the words he or she knows with you.

2. Reread the story taking turns, alternating readers between sentences or pages.

Text Comprehension: Discussion Time

1. Ask your child to retell the sequence of events in the story.

2. To check comprehension, ask your child the following questions:

- What is the man doing on pages 6–8?
- Why did the boy and girl pick up the garbage?
- Have you ever been the new kid at school or in the neighborhood? How did it feel? If you haven't been the new kid, how do you think it would feel?

WORD LIST

A *Friend for Dear Dragon* uses the 67 words listed below.

This list can be used to practice reading the words that appear in the text. You may wish to write the words on index cards and use them to help your child build automatic word recognition. Regular practice with these words will enhance your child's fluency in reading connected text.

a	eat	I	oh	us
am		in	on	
and	for	is	one	want
are	friend	it	out	we
at	fun			what
		like	play	who
big	get	little	pretty	will
but	go	look		with
	good		run	work
can		man		
car	happy	me	see	yes
come	have	my	something	you
	he			
dear	help	no	that	
did	here	not	thing	
do	home	now	this	
dragon	house		to	
	how		too	
			two	

ABOUT THE AUTHOR Margaret Hillert has written over 80 books for children who are just learning to read. Her books have been translated into many different languages and over a million children throughout the world have read her books. She first started writing poetry as a child and has continued to write for children and adults throughout her life. A first grade teacher for 34 years, Margaret is now retired from teaching and lives in Michigan where she likes to write, take walks in the morning, and care for her three cats.

Photograph by Glenna Washburn

ABOUT THE ADVISER Shannon Cannon contributed the activities pages that appear in this book. Shannon serves as a literacy consultant and provides staff development to help improve reading instruction. She is a frequent presenter at educational conferences and workshops. Prior to this she worked as an elementary school teacher and as president of a curriculum publishing company.